Noah's So Noisy

Published in paperback in 2016 by Wayland
Text © Wayland 2016
Illustrations © Jack Hughes 2016

Wayland
An imprint of Hachette Children's Group
Part of Hodder & Stoughton
Carmelite House, 50 Victoria Embankment
London EC4Y 0DZ

Commissioning Editor: Victoria Brooker
Design: Lisa Peacock and Alyssa Peacock

British Library Cataloguing in Publication Data
Heneghan, Judith.
Noah's SO noisy. -- (Dragon School)
1. Etiquette--Pictorial works--Juvenile fiction.
2. Children's stories--Pictorial works.
I. Title II. Series III. Hughes, Jack.
823.9'2-dc23

ISBN: 978 0 7502 8363 2

10 9 8 7 6 5 4 3 2 1

Printed in China

MIX
Paper from
responsible sources
FSC
www.fsc.org
FSC® C104740

Wayland is a division of Hachette Children's Group,
an Hachette UK Company
www.hachette.co.uk

Noah's SO Noisy

Written by Judith Heneghan
Illustrated by Jack Hughes

WAYLAND

Noah was a noisy dragon. When he walked through the forest, he always stamped his feet.

When he crashed through the bushes, all the birds squawked and squeaked.

He roared more loudly than any of his friends. They always heard him coming. 'Noah's here!' they'd say, before he stepped into the clearing.

Noah didn't mind.
He loved making an entrance.

Playing games with Noah was interesting.
When his friends played 'Sleeping Dragons',
he'd flap his wings or thump his tail.
He couldn't keep quiet!

'Hide and Seek' was especially difficult.
When it was Noah's turn to hide,
he'd start whistling, or shout 'HERE I AM!'

Then one day, Brandon brought his new
story book to Dragon School.
'It's got a silver dragon in it!' he said,
showing the book to his friends.

'Ooh!' shouted Noah. 'Will you read it to us?'

'Of course,' replied Brandon. 'But you'll have to be quiet!'

'All right,' sighed Noah. 'I'll try!'

The dragons sat down in a circle
and waited for Brandon to begin.
Brandon took a deep breath.
'Once upon a time...'

'That's a good beginning,' said Noah, to Ruby.
'Do you think this story has pirates in it?'

Ruby wanted to listen to Brandon.
'Shhh!' she hushed, poking Noah with her elbow.
'OUCH!' yelled Noah.

'This is so exciting!' said Noah, thumping his tail on the ground. 'Be quiet!' scolded Jasmine. 'I'm trying to listen to the story!'

But Noah couldn't keep quiet. He stood up and started flapping his wings. 'I WANT TO HEAR ABOUT THE PIRATES!' he shouted.

'I bet the silver dragon meets some pirates
and they find a treasure map and...'

'Stop!' said Brandon, shutting the book.
'Noah, you are SO noisy! You're spoiling the story
for everyone else! Go away and leave us in peace.'

Noah looked a bit surprised. He let out a long whistle, then stomped off into the forest. 'That's better,' said Brandon. He opened his book and got on with reading the story.

Noah watched from the trees. He felt a bit sad. Being quiet was hard, but he did want to hear the rest of the story.

He decided he would try to be quiet.
How did the other dragons do it?

First, he crept up behind a tree. Instead of yelling out 'HERE I AM!' or 'COME AND FIND ME!' he clamped his mouth shut and didn't say a word.

Then he stepped
into the clearing.
Instead of thumping his
tail or stamping his feet,
he tip-toed quietly across the grass.

When he reached the others, he stood
still as a statue and didn't whisper or wriggle.

Brandon was just reaching the end of the story.
'...So the pirates shared their treasure with the silver dragon, and they all lived happily ever after!'

The clearing fell silent for a moment.
Then Noah tapped Brandon quietly on the shoulder.
'Is that the end?' he whispered.

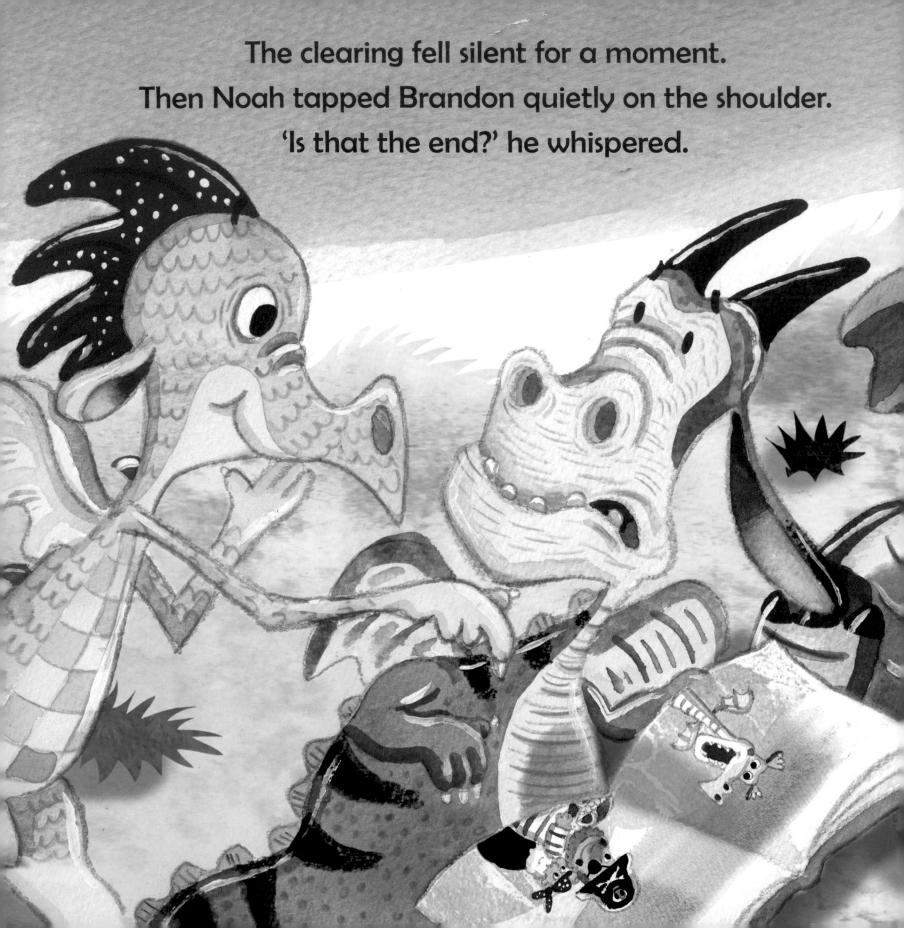

'Aaaargh!' roared his three friends, jumping up in surprise. 'We didn't hear you coming!' exclaimed Jasmine.

'I've been practising keeping quiet,' said Noah.
'I'm sorry for being noisy while you were reading.'

Brandon grinned. 'Shall I read the story again?'
'Yes please,' answered Noah, 'and this time
I promise to listen!'